"Come and meet Rocky," Jack

Ellie and Mum exchanged a
the perfect name, Ellie thought to herself. *Dad is
a rock star, after all!*

They followed Jack up a slope, and he held
the door open as they went into another set
of pens. Ellie gave an excited cry. Mum and
Rachel peered over her shoulder.

In the cage was a group of tiny black-and-
tan puppies with soft-looking fur. One of them
galloped over, a toy in his mouth. He dropped
it in front of the pen door and grinned up at
them. "Ahhhh!" Mum, Rachel and Ellie all
said at the same time.

His paws and chin were brown, and there
were two little brown spots above his eyebrows.
He was small and chubby, with a round belly
and a pointy little tail that wagged back and
forth happily as they looked down at him.

"This is Rocky," Jack smiled.

Have you read all these books in the
Battersea Dogs & Cats home series?

BAILEY'S story

CHESTER'S story

RUSTY'S story

MAX'S story

DAISY'S story

MISTY'S story

STELLA'S story

HUEY'S story

COSMO'S story

ANGEL'S story

ALFIE'S story

COCO'S story

PETAL'S story

BERTIE'S story

SUZY'S story

JESSIE'S story

BRUNO'S story

OSCAR'S story

BUSTER'S story

SNOWY'S story

BUDDY and HOLLY'S story

SPARKLE and BELLE'S story

PIPPIN'S story

ROCKY'S story

ROCKY'S
story

by

Sarah Hawkins

Illustrated by Artful Doodlers

Puzzle Illustrations by Jason Chapman

RED FOX

BATTERSEA DOGS & CATS HOME: ROCKY'S STORY
A RED FOX BOOK 978 1 782 95309 8

First published in Great Britain by Red Fox,
an imprint of Random House Children's Publishers
A Random House Group Company

This edition published 2014

1 3 5 7 9 10 8 6 4 2

The Random House Group Limited supports the Forest Stewardship
Council® (FSC®), the leading international forest-certification organisation.
Our books carrying the FSC label are printed on FSC®-certified paper.
FSC is the only forest-certification scheme supported by the leading
environmental organisations, including Greenpeace. Our paper procurement
policy can be found at www.randomhouse.co.uk/environment.

MIX
Paper from
responsible sources
FSC® C016897

Set in 13/20 Stone Informal

Red Fox Books are published by Random House Children's Publishers,
61–63 Uxbridge Road, London W5 5SA

www.randomhousechildrens.co.uk
www.randomhouse.co.uk
www.battersea.org.uk

Addresses for companies within The Random House Group Limited
can be found at: www.randomhouse.co.uk/offices.htm

THE RANDOM HOUSE GROUP Limited Reg. No. 954009

A CIP catalogue record for this book is available from the British Library.

Printed and bound in Great Britain by
CPI Group (UK) Ltd, Croydon, CR0 4YY

Turn to page **93** for lots
of information on the
Battersea Dogs & Cats Home,
plus some cool activities!

🐾 🐾 🐾 🐾

Meet the stars of the Battersea Dogs & Cats Home series to date . . .

Bailey

Chester

Misty

Max

Daisy

Rusty

Snowy

Stella

Huey

Angel

Alfie

Cosmo

Coco

Buddy and Holly

Petal

Bertie

Suzy

Jessie

Bruno

Oscar

Sparkle and Belle

Pippin

Buster

Jazz and Bo

Rocky

Dad on Tour

"That's the last one," Dad said, stacking a drum in the back of his battered old van.

Ellie crossed her arms as she stood watching on the front doorstep. She put his drumsticks in her back pocket. *Maybe if he doesn't have them, he won't go.*

"Don't pout, babe." Dad came over

and grabbed the drumsticks out of her pocket. "Almost forgot these!" He kissed her on the top of her head and put the drumsticks in with the rest of his kit, then slammed the van door shut.

The Day Trippers! the doors of the van said, in peeling blue letters. Ellie looked down at her T-shirt, which had the same name on it, along with a picture of the band. Her dad's face, looking a bit

younger and funny without his beard, stared back at her. She stuck her tongue out at it.

"I just don't know why you have to go away in the summer holidays," she said. "You should be at home with me and Mum and Rachel. Why can't you have a job in an office like everyone else's dad?"

Dad laughed. "You know I love being a musician, babe. Soon, when you're a bit older, you and Mum and Rachel can come with me on tour. It's so much fun. The fans in Germany love us."

"Not as much as we do," Ellie muttered. She sat down on the doorstep and started making a chain with the daisies that were growing through the cracks in the paving stones.

"Oh, come on, grumpy-chops!" Dad pulled her into a massive hug. "I know what you need. KISS ATTACK!" He started planting kisses all over her face, making Ellie wriggle and squirm as his beard tickled her.

"Stop!" Ellie laughed. It was impossible to be cross during a kiss attack!

Dad pretended to find a guitar-pick behind her ear, and ruffled her long blonde hair. Then he leaned through the open front door. "Judy! I'm going!" he shouted up the stairs. Mum ran down and flung herself into Dad's arms.

Rachel, Ellie's big sister, followed after her carrying a book. "Bye, Dad," she said, reaching up for a hug.

"You're even going to miss Rachel's birthday!" Ellie protested. "Your own daughter! Isn't she more important than your fans?"

Dad's smile dropped. "Of COURSE she is," he said seriously. "So are you, and Mum. But the fans pay to see the band, which pays the bills, which means that I have to go and do gigs even when I'd rather be at home with my three girls."

He turned to Rachel and gave her a

big hug. "You know I'm sorry to be missing your birthday, Rach."

"I don't mind," Rachel said.

Ellie knew she did really. Even though she was older, Rachel was much quieter and shyer than Ellie was. She'd never say it, but Ellie knew her sister hated it when Dad was away just as much as she did.

"We'll have a special second birthday for you when Dad gets home," Mum said brightly. She gave Dad a huge hug and a kiss. "You look exactly the same as when we met," she said dreamily. "My rock star!"

Ellie groaned and Mum laughed, putting her arms around both girls.

"Wave goodbye to your dad!"

Dad kissed Rachel and Ellie on the head and gave Mum one more hug. "See you in a couple of months, my beautiful girls!" he called, getting in the van. He started the engine and turned the radio on, blaring out music.

"Bye! Bye!" Rachel and Mum called. They waved until the van had gone down to the end of the road and, with a *beep-beep* of the horn, turned out of sight.

There was a second's silence, and Ellie felt a sad, flat feeling take over her. She hated being left behind. "Well!" Mum said in a cheerful voice. "What shall we have for tea?"

Ellie wrenched herself out of her mum's arms and ran upstairs to her bedroom. As she threw herself onto her bed, her foot knocked over the pink guitar Dad had given her for her last birthday, and she didn't even bother picking it up. She pushed a pillow against her stinging eyes.

I'm not going to cry, Ellie thought to herself fiercely. *I'm going to make a plan – a plan to get Dad to stay at home for good!*

A Birthday Wish

Ellie gave a groan of frustration and
dropped the guitar onto her bed.

"It sounds OK to me," Rachel said
without looking up from her book.

"It's not," Ellie said. "I just can't
get this chord right. I wish Dad was
here to help me."

She glanced up at her sister, who was curled up on the windowsill reading a book. "Do you want to come and play outside?" she asked hopefully.

"Nah," Rachel said, turning a page. "I'm reading."

"You're *always* reading!" Ellie replied. She got up and went over to the window. "It's nice and sunny out there . . ."

Rachel didn't reply. Ellie gave an exaggerated sigh. "What are you reading, anyway?"

She tugged on the book and Rachel showed her the cover. It had a tiny puppy on it, looking shivery in the snow.

"It's about a puppy called Patch,"

Rachel explained, her eyes sparkling. "It's so exciting. He's lost and his owner is really sad."

Ellie looked at the picture of the puppy and had an idea. "That's it!" she shrieked.

"That's what?" Rachel said confusedly.

"That's what we need to make Dad stay at home more!" Ellie exclaimed. "A dog! Dad loves dogs. If we had one he wouldn't ever want to go away on tour!"

"I don't think a dog is going to make much difference, Els," Rachel said sensibly. "After all, Dad has us and he still has to go away."

Ellie felt a flood of disappointment.

"But having a puppy of our own *would* be nice . . ." Rachel added.

"Yes!" Ellie said. "I'd have someone to play with."

"We could look after it together!" Rachel said excitedly. "Maybe I can ask Mum for one for my birthday?"

"Yes! She can't say no if it's for your birthday!" Ellie jumped up, then stopped as she had another thought. "Oh, but then it would be yours, not mine," she said sadly.

Rachel giggled. "I'll ask if I can have the dog for both of us, silly."

Ellie flung herself at her sister and gave her a massive hug.

"Let's ask Mum now." Rachel jumped up. "Sorry, Patch," she laughed as she left her book on the windowsill. "I've got to ask about a real dog!"

*

Mum was drawing in her studio downstairs, leaning over her desk with chalks of every colour lined up next to her. "What's up, girls?" she asked, wiping her hands on a cloth as they came in.

Ellie rushed over. "We've had a brilliant idea," she said, suddenly feeling nervous. *What if Mum said no?*

"Oh yeah? What is it?" Mum asked, pulling Ellie onto her lap to give her a hug.

"Well, it's for Rachel's birthday, really." Ellie turned to her big sister. "It'd be the best present EVER!"

"A puppy!" Rachel said.

"A puppy!" Mum echoed in surprise. "And this was your idea, was it, Rachel?"

"Well, it was Ellie's idea, but it's really, really what I want," Rachel said. "And I don't mind sharing with Ellie, even if it is my birthday present."

"Hmm." Mum swivelled her chair thoughtfully. "A dog is such a lot of responsibility, girls. It's not something that you can get for a birthday or Christmas present and then forget about, it's a living creature just like you, and you need to look after it and give it lots of love every single day. You wouldn't like it if I didn't feed you, would you?"

"We would feed it!" Ellie protested.

"Who would take it for walks?" Mum asked.

"We both would," Rachel promised.

"And Dad would love it!" Ellie said. "He's always wanted a dog but he couldn't have one because he's been on the road all the time."

Mum smiled. "I will think about it, OK?"

Ellie felt her shoulders drop with disappointment. "That means no."

"No." Mum playfully flicked Ellie's bottom with the cloth. "That means I will think about it. And it's not your birthday anyway, so I think you should be thanking your big sister for wanting to share with you."

"Thanks, Rach," Ellie said. "Come on, let's go and do some research on the internet. We can find out all about being *responsible owners*."

Mum laughed as Ellie dragged her sister away.

"Do you think we'll be allowed?" Ellie

whispered as they closed the door.

"I don't know." Rachel shook her head. "But I hope so." She looked dreamily into the air. "That sort of thing only happens in books – it would be a birthday wish come true!"

A Doggy Decision

"More hot *dogs*, Rachel?" Ellie offered.

"Yes please, I *love* dogs!" Rachel giggled.

"So do I," Ellie replied loudly.

"All right, all right," Mum sighed. "No more dog conversations, please!" They were sitting around the dinner table. Ellie and Rachel had thought about dogs all afternoon. They'd looked up different breeds on the computer, and then they'd gone out in the garden and, for once, Rachel had joined in one of Ellie's games – pretending that they were the girls in Rachel's book, looking for their lost puppy in the snow. They'd even asked Mum if they could have hot dogs for dinner!

"I've made a decision," Mum said. Ellie sat bolt upright. Rachel leaned forward, her eyes wide. Mum took a bite of hot dog and chewed slowly.

"What?" Ellie asked.

Rachel crossed her fingers.

"I just don't think it's fair that you

should have a dog as a birthday present, Rachel," Mum said.

"But Mum, it's what I want!" Rachel protested.

"No." Mum spoke firmly. "I don't like the idea of an animal being given as a gift. And you shouldn't have to share your present."

Ellie looked down at her plate sadly. She'd really thought that they were going to be allowed a dog.

"But . . ." Mum continued. "You girls have shown me that you're willing to be responsible and help out. And I must admit I get a bit lonely while Dad's away too. Having a dog would be brilliant."

Ellie held her breath. For once she couldn't speak.

"You mean . . . ?" Rachel paused, not daring to finish her sentence.

"We can get a dog!" Mum said.

Ellie jumped out of her seat and rocketed around the table. Rachel jumped up too, and they both raced over to Mum.

"I can't believe it!" Ellie squealed. "A dog, a real dog of our very own!"

"I've been looking on the internet this afternoon as well." Mum grinned, getting out her phone. "There's a rescue centre not too far from here called Battersea Dogs & Cats Home. They look after all kinds of dogs and cats that need a family of their own. I thought we could go there."

"Does Dad know?" Ellie asked.

"No, I thought we could keep it as a nice surprise for when he gets back," Mum told them.

Ellie had a thought and grinned at her sister. Rachel smiled back and gave a nod.

"This deserves something really special," Ellie told Mum.

"DOUBLE KISS ATTACK!" the sisters shouted, pouncing on Mum and showering her with kisses.

*

"Hold on!" The picture got clearer and Dad's face appeared on the computer screen. "Girls!" he cried. "How are you? I miss you so much!"

"We're OK," Rachel told him. Ellie wriggled in the chair next to her sister. She hated keeping secrets – she was dying to tell Dad about the puppy.

"Where are you?" Rachel asked.

"We're in Germany." Dad said. "The tour's going really well, but I'm so tired! I can't jump around like I used to. What have you two been up to?"

Ellie and Rachel shared a smile.

"Oh, reading," Rachel said, grinning at Ellie.

"What about you, Els?" Dad said.

"You're awfully quiet today. Are you OK?"

Ellie was bursting to tell him. Rachel kicked her foot under the table where Dad couldn't see.

"I'm OK," Ellie told him. "I've been reading too." It wasn't a lie because she had been doing lots of reading – all about dogs!

"Well done, babe, that's great," Dad said. "It's good to see you two doing something together. Well, better go, it's nine o'clock over here and we've got to go and do our sound-check. Love you – bye!"

"OK, bye!" the girls called, closing the laptop.

"I thought you were going to ruin the surprise and tell him!" Rachel squealed.

"I nearly did!" Ellie confessed. "I couldn't think of anything to say that wasn't about the puppy!" She felt a bit bad about not telling Dad, but at least one bit was true . . . she and Rachel would be doing something together – looking after a puppy!

Battersea Dogs & Cats Home

"Blinking sat nav!" Mum complained as they turned another corner. "It should be around here somewhere."

"Mum!" Ellie shouted as she caught sight of a big blue sign showing a cat and a dog curled up together. "Look, over there!"

"Brilliant!" Mum said, pulling into a side street and parking. "I thought we were going to go round in circles all day long."

"Come on, Rachel, we're here." Ellie leaned over to the front seat and nudged her sister. "It's time to find our puppy! I don't know how you can read at a time like this. Aren't you excited?"

"Of course I am!" Rachel replied. "But I'm at a good bit."

"Meeting our puppy is far more interesting!" Ellie laughed. "Come on!"

She scrambled out of the car
into the sunshine. It was bright
and hot outside. Ellie had
put on her favourite
clothes to meet the
puppy – pretty pink
sandals with flowers on,
pink shorts and a T-shirt
with a pink guitar and
musical notes on it. Rachel
was wearing a long dress, and
Mum had shorts and her
favourite wedge heels on.

Mum grabbed them
both by the hands as they
went in. "I'm nervous!" she said.
"Isn't that silly?"

"I'm nervous too!" Ellie told her.
"I wonder what our puppy's going to
be like!"

Mum squeezed her hand as they went into the reception area.

"I'm Ms Cannon and these are my daughters, Ellie and Rachel Manning," Mum said to the lady at the desk. "We've got an appointment."

"Ms Cannon?" A smiley man with dark blond hair came over and shook Mum's hand. "I'm Jack. Come over to our interview rooms and we'll have a little chat."

Jack led them

into a little room with a table and chairs,
and everyone sat down.

"Now, nothing to worry about." Jack
smiled. "I just want to ask you some
questions about your lifestyle and your
house to make sure that we get the perfect
dog for you. Are you two excited?" he
asked Ellie and Rachel.

Rachel nodded. "We've been reading all about looking after a puppy," she said.

"We want to be the best dog owners ever!" Ellie added.

"We've got a large garden and lots of space," Mum said. "My partner travels with his band, but I work at home, so there would always be someone around."

"Wow, a band?" Jack grinned. "Are you musical as well?" he asked, nodding at the guitar on Ellie's T-shirt.

"A bit," she said. "Dad's teaching me."

"Well, I think I might have just the puppy for a rock family like you . . . Do you want to come and meet him?"

"Yes, please!" Ellie cried. Rachel nodded frantically.

Jack led them through a blue door into the kennels. Ellie looked around curiously as they passed lots of pens with a dog in each one.

A big shaggy brown dog started barking loudly as they went past, making her jump. Mum squeezed her hand and bent down to whisper in her ear. "That one's noisy like you, and that one over there" – she pointed to a little Jack Russell, who was curled up, looking at them with big brown eyes – "is quiet like Rachel!"

Ellie grinned as she looked from one dog to another. In the third pen there was a big dog with brown-and-white patches, and bright blue eyes. As Ellie looked at her, the dog trotted over and rubbed her head against Ellie's hand.

"Hi," Ellie breathed.

She glanced over at Rachel, who was fussing over a little white dog in a nearby pen.

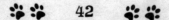

Rachel looked up, her eyes bright.

Ellie felt a jolt of worry. *What if she and Rachel picked different dogs? They always liked such different things, and if they couldn't agree, maybe Mum would say they weren't allowed one after all . . .*

Mum caught her eye and came over. "You OK, darling?" she asked.

"How are we going to know which one is the right one?" Ellie asked.

"We'll know the dog for us when we see him or her," Mum reassured her. "If he's not here today, we'll come back another day. OK?"

Ellie nodded, feeling a bit better.

"Come and meet Rocky," Jack called.

Ellie and Mum exchanged a glance. *Rocky is the perfect name*, Ellie thought to herself. *Dad is a rock star, after all!*

They followed Jack up a slope, and he held the door open as they went into another set of pens. Ellie gave an excited cry as Mum and Rachel peered over her shoulder.

In the cage as a group of tiny black-and-tan puppies with soft-looking fur.

One of them galloped over, a toy in his mouth. He dropped it in front of the pen door and grinned up at them. "Ahhhh!" Mum, Rachel and Ellie all said at the same time.

His paws and chin were brown, and there were two little brown spots above his eyebrows. He was small and chubby, with a round belly and a pointy little tail that wagged back and forth happily as they looked down at him.

"This is Rocky," Jack smiled.

Rocky

"We've already found homes for all his brothers and sisters," Jack explained. "Rottweilers are very loyal dogs, who absolutely love their families."

Mum nodded. "We used to have a Rottie when I was little, and he was the biggest softie. I've always liked the idea of having another one, one day . . ."

Rocky jumped up at the mesh on the cage, barking tiny high-pitched barks. "*Raff!*"

Ellie and Rachel reached out to stroke him through the wire. "He can't even bark properly yet!" Ellie said in amazement.

"They're only seven weeks old." Jack opened the cage and scooted the puppies inside, then picked up Rocky. "Let's take him into the playroom so you can meet him properly," he suggested.

Mum, Rachel and Ellie followed Jack into a room where there was a sofa and a basket full of dog toys. When he put the puppy down, Rocky galloped over to the toys and picked one up, then trotted back to show it to Ellie and Rachel.

"Hello!" Ellie said in delight, bending down to greet the excited pup.

"We had to hand-rear them because their mother couldn't feed them, so he's very friendly," Jack explained.

Rachel bent down and tried to pick up the toy. Rocky grabbed the other end of it with his little teeth and tugged hard. Rachel giggled and let go. Rocky raced around happily, his tail wagging excitedly. Ellie watched her sister and laughed.

Rocky ran past her and she reached out
to stroke his tiny head. He was so soft!
She glanced up at her family and all her
worries flew away. There were huge smiles
on Mum and Rachel's faces. It looked like
they'd all fallen in love with him!

Rocky shook the toy from side to side,
then dropped it at their feet, grinning up
at them proudly.

"He's adorable!" Mum grinned.

"Oh yes!" Rachel agreed. "He's perfect!"

"He's our puppy," Ellie whispered happily.

*

"Welcome home, Rocky!" Ellie cheered as the car pulled into the driveway.

It was two weeks since they'd first met him, but to Ellie it felt like years! Luckily, there had been lots of things to do before Rocky arrived. A nice lady from Battersea had come round to their house to check that their home was suitable for a puppy. She'd said that everything was fine, and that they could fetch him as soon as he had been given all his vaccinations. On the big day they had all got up early, so they could get to Battersea Dogs & Cats Home as soon as it opened!

"Why don't you take Rocky straight

out into the garden?" Mum suggested as they got out of the car. "It's been a long journey for a little dog, and we don't want any puppy accidents!"

"OK!" Ellie agreed. She carefully carried Rocky round into the back garden. As soon as Rachel shut the garden gate, the little puppy squirmed and wriggled to get down.

Ellie put him down, then she and her sister watched delightedly as he sniffed round all the bushes, poking his nose under everything.

"I still can't believe he's really ours!" Ellie squealed.

"Me neither," Rachel agreed. "He's the cutest thing in the world!"

Once Rocky had done his business, Ellie opened the back door and called him over. "Rocky!"

Rocky ran out of the bushes with one of Mum's gardening gloves hanging out of his mouth.

"Where did you find that?" Ellie laughed. "Come on, I'll show you where your toys are." She stepped inside and Rocky raced after her. But he was too little to get over the step! He put his front paws over and gave a little hop, but his bum was still in the garden.

"Oh Rocky!" Ellie and Rachel were almost crying with laughter as they helped him inside.

"This is where you're going to sleep, Rocky," Ellie said as she and Rachel led him though the back door into the kitchen. They'd set up the dog basket in a cosy corner. They had chosen some new toys especially for him, and put them in his basket.

Rocky jumped in and went over to sniff them. He looked so tiny in the enormous basket that both girls laughed.

Mum came in and smiled at

the funny sight. "He'll grow!" she grinned.

Rocky jumped out of his basket and wandered around the kitchen, giving everything a good sniff.

"No, Rocky," Mum warned as he sniffed at a tea towel hanging over the back of a chair. "That's not yours. Look, your toys are over here."

Mum went to pick him up, but before she could, the little puppy grabbed the tea towel off the chair and ran away with it!

Ellie and Rachel burst out laughing. Having Rocky was going to be lots of fun!

Rachel's Day

"Three, two, one . . ." Mum whispered, lighting the candles on the cake. "Go!"

Ellie strummed on her guitar. "Hap-py birthday to you, hap-py birthday to you!" they sang as they burst into Rachel's bedroom.

Rachel was a lump in the middle of her

bed, the covers over her head, but she stirred at the noise. Ellie jumped onto the end of the bed, still singing. "Happy BIRTHday dear Rachel . . . happy birthday tooooo yooooou."

"*Raff, raff!*" Rocky barked. He tried to jump up on the bed after Ellie, but his little legs were too short. Ellie giggled and picked him up. He raced over the bedcovers, sniffing at them excitedly. When he found Rachel, he barked delightedly and licked her face. "Yuck, Rocky!" Rachel complained, laughing. She sat up sleepily and grinned at Mum and Ellie.

"Blow out your candles!" Mum said, holding out the cake.

Taking a big breath, Rachel blew hard. Mum pulled a knife and some napkins out of her pocket and shoved Rachel over so she could get in the bed next to her.

"Birthday cake for breakfast – don't tell Dad!" Mum grinned, giving Rachel a party hat and plonking one on Ellie's head too.

"OK!" Rachel grinned.

"Do you like it?" Ellie asked her big sister, pointing at the cake. She'd helped Mum decorate it so it looked like Rachel's favourite book.

"*The Secret Garden* . . ." Rachel read the swirly

letters Mum had written in icing. "And there's the garden wall, with ivy, and the garden fork – oh, and the robin too! Thanks!"

"I did the robin." Ellie grinned.

Mum cut them each a bit and they snuggled up in Rachel's bed eating it.

Rocky nosed at Ellie's cake curiously. Ellie broke off the tiniest crumb for him, and he snuffled it out of her hand. He licked his lips, then jumped onto Ellie's lap and tried to grab the rest of her cake off her napkin.

Ellie giggled as she picked up the
wriggly little puppy and put him next to
Rachel on the bed. Rocky snuggled up
to her sister, then started snuffling under
a spare party hat. First he pushed his
nose under it, then his whole head. It
looked like he was wearing it specially!

"Oh, Rocky!" Ellie laughed. "You're the
cutest puppy in the world!"

"Right, time for presents," Mum said
as they finished laughing. Rocky watched
her as she ran to the door and picked up
the pile of presents she'd left there.

"This one's from me and Rocky," Ellie told her. Rachel ripped the paper off excitedly. Ellie grinned as her sister held up the book.

"*How to Train Your Puppy,*" Rachel read. "Thanks!" She reached over to give Ellie a hug.

"Open this one, open this one!" Mum said excitedly.

"You can help, Rocky!" Rachel said as she tore open the package. She held the corner of the wrapping paper out to the friendly little puppy and he grabbed it in his teeth and pulled, his tail wagging so excitedly that he almost fell over.

Inside was a big fluffy toy bunny. "Aw, it's so cute," Rachel said, hugging Mum. "Thank you!"

Meanwhile Rocky was looking at the rabbit excitedly. Ellie recognized that look! "Rocky, no!" she cried, but it was too late. Rocky jumped up, grabbed the toy in his mouth, leaped off the bed and raced away, dragging it behind him!

*

"What do you want to do today, birthday girl?" Mum asked later on when they were all dressed.

"Talk to Dad first!" Rachel raced over to the phone and dialled the number. But there was no answer.

"Never mind," Mum soothed. "He's probably rehearsing. I'm sure he'll call us the second he can."

"It doesn't matter," Rachel mumbled.

Yes it does! Ellie thought crossly. It was bad enough that Dad was away, but now he wasn't even there to sing Rachel happy birthday. It was rubbish!

"I wanted to read my new book anyway," Rachel said, curling up on the beanbag chair with her book.

Ellie knew her big sister was sad.

Rocky seemed to know too, because he went over and started covering Rachel's face with licky kisses, then grabbed one

end of her book with
his mouth and tried
to run away with
it!

"No, Rocky!"
Rachel tried to pull
her book away from
him but he squatted
down and pulled back.

Ellie picked up the cheeky puppy. "You
naughty boy!" she gently scolded him.
The corner of Rachel's new book was
covered in puppy toothmarks! Ellie and
Rachel looked at it and collapsed into
giggles.

"Why don't we take Rocky for a walk?"
Mum suggested. "Come on, I've just
remembered a little park we haven't
been to since you were babies. It'll be
like the Secret Garden, Rach!"

Rachel glanced at her book.

"You can bring your book too! Come on, it's a birthday adventure!" Ellie added.

Mum glanced at her watch. "We have to be back at three anyway . . . I've got a birthday surprise for you!"

"OK," Rachel agreed. "Besides, I think Rocky understands the word *walk* . . ."

Rocky was looking up at them expectantly. His ears had pricked up and his eyes were bright.

"Walk?" Ellie said again.

"*Raff!*" Rocky agreed.

Rachel giggled, and Ellie smiled. With Rocky's help, today was going to be a good birthday after all!

Puppy Adventure

"Is the surprise a bike? Or a new guitar?" Ellie asked as they got out of the car.

"No and no," Mum replied. "And would you stop guessing? Honestly, it's not even *your* present! Rachel's nowhere near as excited as you are!" Ellie looked in the back of the car and grinned. Rachel was already reading her puppy-care book, and Rocky was sitting on her lap, looking at the book like he was reading too. Every so often he'd try and eat the pages.

Ellie held Rocky's lead tightly as they got out of the car. They'd taken him for a walk every day since he'd come home, but this was the first time they'd brought him to a park. Ellie still couldn't believe that she was walking their very own puppy! She felt so proud as they walked in with the little puppy racing along in front of them.

"Can we let him off his lead, Mum?" Ellie asked.

"Hmmm," Mum said. "I don't know. He does know his name. Rocky!" Rocky turned to look at her. "What does your book say, Rach?"

They stopped under a big tree while

Rachel found the right page. The park was so pretty, with grassy spaces, trees in neat lines and colourful flowers blooming everywhere. It was so hot and sunny that there were lots of people out, lying on the grass, playing games, and they could hear an ice-cream van tinkling in the distance.

While Mum and
Rachel looked at the
book, Ellie and Rocky
wandered about. There
was a cute signpost
with lots of arrows pointing in
different directions, and Ellie
took Rocky over to read what it said.
Flower Garden, Fountain, Orchard, Maze . . .

"Ooh, Mum, Can we go to the maze?"
Ellie called.

"Maybe later," Mum replied. "Bring
Rocky over here . . . The book says he
needs to be a bit older before he's let off
his lead because he's still so young; he's
easily distracted," she said. "But he needs
to learn to come when he's called, so we
can practise with his lead on."

"OK!" Ellie agreed.

"If he comes when he's called, we

should give him a treat and make a big fuss of him. Here, Ellie, you try first." Mum got some treats out of her pocket and gave them to Ellie.

Mum held onto the lead loosely. Ellie patted her knees and called him. "Rocky! Rocky!"

The puppy bounded straight over to her, dragging Mum behind him, his eyes wide and his tongue hanging out. He looked up at Ellie and put his head to one side curiously.

Ellie gave him a treat and bent down to hug him. "Good boy!" she exclaimed, stroking him all over.

Rocky wriggled delightedly in her arms.

He didn't know he was being taught; he thought it was a fun new game!

Mum and Rachel tried it too, and Rocky came every time he was called.

"Well done, Rocky." Ellie reached down to stroke his velvety ears. "You'll be

running around on your own before you know it."

Ellie took Rocky's lead, and they carried on with their walk.

"It says that because he's so little he won't want to be far away from us," Rachel read out loud from her book as she walked along.

"Watch out!" Ellie grabbed her sister as she almost walked into a signpost.

Rocky pulled on the lead, stopping to sniff things but always turning back to make sure they were right behind them.

Ellie grabbed Mum's hand and Mum
took Rachel's, and the three of them
went along happily swinging their arms

together. *The only thing that would make
this perfect would be if Dad was here too,*
Ellie thought, looking at a dad and a
little boy nearby.

As she watched them, they both looked

up at something in the sky.
A flash of colour caught
Ellie's eye, and she saw their
bright yellow kite swooping
and dipping in the air. As she
watched, the wind wrenched the
kite out of the boy's hands. It was
swept along, the boy racing after it.

"*Raff, raff!*" Rocky barked excitedly.

The kite was lifted high in the air, then
swooped low overhead.

Rocky jumped around Ellie's legs,
tangling her up with his lead.

"Hold on," Ellie giggled.
She hopped one
of her legs
over the
lead, but
as she
did, the

kite crashed to the ground. At the same time, Rocky pulled on his lead – and Ellie toppled over!

The lead flew out of her hands, and Rocky galloped over to the kite, his little legs running so fast they were almost a blur, his tongue hanging out in excitement.

"Rocky!" Ellie called, but this time he didn't come back. He picked up the kite in his mouth and ran off, just like he had with the tea towel and Rachel's present.

Ellie felt full of dread. "Rocky!" she shouted as she started to run after him.

"Rocky, come back!" Mum and Rachel ran after him too, calling his name, but the excited puppy didn't listen.

Ellie ran as fast as she could. Mum and Rachel fell behind, but Ellie didn't stop. She was panting too much to call for Rocky and she had a sharp pain in her side, but she kept her eyes on him. He was too little to be on his own – anything could happen to him.

Rocky was playing with the kite like one of his toys, shaking it excitedly as

he ran along. He raced between some trees and past some thick bushes, turning left and right. He turned a corner by some pink flowers, and for a second Ellie couldn't see him. She was really tired now, but she made her legs keep going. She couldn't lose her puppy!

As she turned the corner she gave a sigh of relief. Rocky was standing in the middle of a little clearing, giving the kite a good shake.

"Rocky!" Ellie managed to gasp out.

Rocky looked up and his tail wagged happily. "*Raff!*" he barked, as if he was saying "Look what I've got!"

"Oh, Rocky!" Ellie said as she picked up his lead. "You scared me! I thought I was never going to see you again!" She sat down on the ground next to her naughty puppy while she got her breath back.

Rocky left the kite and came and jumped up onto her lap for a cuddle.

"I'd better get you back to Mum and Rachel," Ellie said as she stroked his floppy ears and he nuzzled into her hand. "They'll be worried."

She looked around. There were thick dark green hedges all around her. "Er, Rocky," She said, rubbing her fingers through his soft coat anxiously. "Where are we?"

Maze Mistake

As Ellie looked at the hedges all around her, she tried not to panic. They must be in the maze! Suddenly she remembered her phone. She'd begged Mum for one for ages, and she'd finally got one for emergencies. She'd just phone Mum, who would come and find them. But when she

tried to call, her mobile wouldn't work.
There was no signal – probably because
of the maze. Ellie put it back in her pocket
and sighed.

What would Rachel do? she thought to
herself. Her big sister was always calm.

 Ellie looked down at
Rocky, who grinned up
at her expectantly,
his eyes bright and
his pink tongue
hanging out cheekily.
"Let's go back the
way we came," Ellie decided. But when
she looked from one leafy pathway to the
other, they both looked exactly the same.
When she rushed in she'd been watching
Rocky, not looking where she was going!

Ellie looked from left to right, then
from right to left. "Ummm, I think it was

this way," she said. "Come on, Rocky." The puppy trotted happily at her heels as she led him down the leafy corridor.

They made one turn, then another. Whenever they came to a turn, Ellie guessed which way to go. Finally they came to a clearing . . . with a yellow kite on the floor. They were back exactly where they'd started!

Ellie tried to call Mum again, but the phone still wasn't working. Then she looked at the time and groaned. Mum had planned a surprise for three o'clock and it was nearly two now. She was going to ruin her own sister's birthday!

"Oh, Rocky!" Ellie sighed. "What are we going to do?"

Rocky pulled her over to the kite and Ellie tugged on the lead crossly. "Leave it alone, Rocky. That's what got us into this mess!"

Rocky grabbed the kite in his teeth and started shaking it. As it moved, Ellie caught sight of the kite string. It was trailing out behind it – round the corner! That must be the direction they'd come in. "That's it!" She gasped. "Well done, Rocky!"

Ellie picked up the kite and started walking along, following the string as they went. It led them round the corner, past the pink flowers.

The kite string was long, tangled and caught on the hedges. Ellie collected it up as she went.

Rocky galloped along proudly with the kite in his mouth.

As Ellie turned a corner, she could see the end of the string trailing in front of her. She glanced around, hoping to see the entrance. Then she heard a call.

"Ell-ie! Roc-ky!"

It was Mum!

"Mum!" Ellie yelled back. "Over here!"

Mum ran round the corner, followed
by Rachel, the dad and the little boy, and
swept her up into a fierce hug. "Oh, thank
goodness you caught him," she gasped.

Rachel knelt down and made a fuss of Rocky.

"I followed him in here, but then I couldn't find the way out!" Ellie explained.

Rachel grinned at her sister and pointed to the big signpost at the entrance to the maze. "You should read sometimes, Ellie," she laughed.

Ellie giggled. "We'll have to teach Rocky to read – does it tell us how to do that in your training book?"

"No time for that now," Mum said, hurriedly giving the kite back to the little boy. "We have to go – we're going to be late for your birthday surprise!"

Surprise!

Mum rushed them all the way home. They burst into the house, but nothing seemed that surprising. In fact, everything seemed just the same as it had when they'd left. Rocky raced over to his food bowl and started happily munching on his dry dog food.

"Where's the surprise?" Ellie asked
indignantly.

"You'll just have to wait a minute,"
Mum said with a mysterious smile.

Just then there was a *beep-beep* from
outside. Ellie and
Rachel looked at
each other in
amazement.

"That sounds
like—" Rachel
started.

"But it can't be—" Ellie interrupted.

"Dad!" they both shrieked together.

Shutting the kitchen door so Rocky
didn't run off for another adventure,
the girls sped to the front door and flung
it open.

Dad's van pulled into the drive. The
second it stopped, he jumped out of

the driver's seat and picked Rachel up, flinging her round in a big circle.

"Happy birthday, babe!" he bellowed as she squealed in delight. "And hello, Els – give your old dad a hug."

Ellie rushed over to squeeze him round his middle. "What are you *doing* here?" she asked.

"You're meant to be in Germany!" Rachel added in amazement.

"Our lead singer got ill and lost his voice so we had to cancel the rest of the tour," Dad told them. "I drove all night long so I could be here for your birthday."

As Mum appeared in the doorway, Dad knelt down and put his arms around the girls. "It was too hard to be away from you on your birthday, Rach. I want to be here for all your birthdays, and weekends, and school holidays. I want to be home

all the time, with my girls. And I'm getting a bit old for touring anyway." He grinned at Ellie. "I met a guy on tour who sets up recording studios. I thought that I could put one in the attic and work from home – so I won't have to go away so much."

"Really?" Ellie gasped. "You're not going on tour again?"

"Not until you're both old enough to come with me." Dad beamed. "If that's OK."

Mum clapped her hands in delight. "That's brilliant."

Rachel's eyes filled with happy tears and she buried her face in Dad's shoulder.

"Hey, no tears," he said. "I know what will make you smile – presents!"

They went inside and Dad gave Mum a massive hug. "Best birthday surprise ever," Mum told him.

"Hey, you haven't seen what this is yet." Dad gave Rachel a brightly coloured bag. She opened it and pulled out a notebook with puppies on it.

"If I'm going to have a studio here I'm going to need some new songs," Dad said. "Maybe you can do some writing as well as reading. I know how much you like puppies, too . . ."

Rachel and Ellie looked at each other and burst out laughing.

"We've got a surprise as well, Dad," Ellie giggled. "A big one. And it's in the kitchen."

Dad looked really confused. Ellie swung open the door, and Rocky ran out, dragging a tea towel behind him.

"Rocky!" Ellie shrieked as she chased after him. "Give that back!"

That evening, as they all sat in the lounge, Ellie looked round at her family

happily. Dad had taught her how to play
the chord she was stuck on, and was now
gently playing the guitar while Mum sang
along. For once Rachel wasn't reading,
but was sitting with her new notepad,
chewing the end of a pen thoughtfully.

Best of all, Rocky was curled up asleep on Ellie's lap, giving little puppy snores. He was completely tired out after his adventurous day.

"Ellie," Rachel whispered, being careful not to wake Rocky up, "I know what kind of song I'm going to write – one about a dog and a kite!"

Ellie grinned. Dad was home for good, and she had a puppy. It was more than she had wished for. Ellie gently stroked Rocky's soft fur and felt happier than she ever had before. Then she picked up the *How to Train Your Puppy* book and started reading. Rocky was absolutely perfect just the way he was – but he still had a lot to learn!

Read on for lots more . . .

❧ ❧ ❧ ❧

The inspirations for ROCKY'S story
is the real-life dog who lived
at Battersea Dogs & Cats Home:

NAME: Star

BREED: Rottweiler

LIKES: Sitting on your
lap, paddling in the sea,
bouncing

DISLIKES: Going on a
diet, fireworks

Battersea Dogs & Cats Home

Battersea Dogs & Cats Home is a charity that aims never to turn away a dog or cat in need of our help. We reunite lost dogs and cats with their owners; when we can't do this, we care for them until new homes can be found for them; and we educate the public about responsible pet ownership. Every year the Home takes in around 9,000 dogs and cats. In addition to the site in southwest London, the Home also has two other centres based at Old Windsor, Berkshire, and Brands Hatch, Kent.

The original site in Holloway

History

The Temporary Home for Lost and Starving Dogs was originally opened in a stable yard in Holloway in 1860 by Mary Tealby after she found a starving puppy in the street. There was no one to look after him, so she took him home. She was so worried about the other dogs wandering the streets that she opened the Temporary Home for Lost and Starving Dogs. The Home was established to help to look after them all and find them new owners.

Sadly Mary Tealby died in 1865, aged sixty-four, and little more is known about her, but her good work was continued. In 1871 the Home moved to its present site in Battersea, and was renamed the Dogs' Home Battersea.

Some important dates for the Home:

1883 – Battersea start taking in cats.

1914 – 100 sledge dogs are housed at the Hackbridge site, in preparation for Ernest Shackleton's second Antarctic expedition.

1956 – Queen Elizabeth II becomes patron of the Home.

2004 – Red the Lurcher's night-time antics become world famous when he is caught on camera regularly escaping from his kennel and liberating his canine chums for midnight feasts.

2007 – The BBC broadcast *Animal Rescue Live* from the Home for three weeks from mid-July to early August.

2012 – Paul O'Grady's hit ITV1 series and Christmas Special, *For the Love of Dogs*, follows the stories of many Battersea dogs.

The process for re-homing a dog or a cat

When a lost dog or cat arrives, Battersea's Lost Dogs & Cats Line works hard to try to find the animal's owners. If, after seven days, they have not been able to reunite them, the search for a new home can begin.

The Home works hard to find caring, permanent new homes for all the lost and unwanted dogs and cats.

Dogs and cats have their own characters and so staff at the Home will spend time getting to know every dog and cat. This helps decide the type of home the dog or cat needs.

There are three stages of the re-homing process at Battersea Dogs & Cats Home. Battersea's re-homing team wants to find you the perfect pet: sometimes this can take a while, so please be patient while we search for your new friend!

1 Register details

2 Match

3 Leaving with your new pet

Have a look at our website: **http://www.battersea.org.uk/dogs/ rehoming/index.html** for more details!

Fingerprint dogs and cats.

Thumb print over corner of scrap paper and remove to leave white triangle for nose and mouth.

Stick-on eyes: Hole-punched pieces of paper with dots marked in the centres.

Or use white paint to make eyes and tummy.

Making a Mask

Copy these faces onto a piece of paper
andask an adult to help you cut them out.

Jokes

WARNING – you might get serious belly-ache after reading these!

What do you get when you cross a dog and a phone?
A golden receiver!

What is a vampire's favourite dog?
A bloodhound!

What kind of pets lie around the house?
Car-pets!

What's worse than raining cats and dogs?
Hailing elephants!

What do you call a dog that is a librarian?
A hush-puppy!

What do you get when you cross a mean dog and a computer?
A mega-bite!

Why couldn't the Dalmatian hide from his pal?
Because he was already spotted!

What do you do with a blue Burmese?
Try and cheer it up!

Why did the cat join the Red Cross?
Because she wanted to be a first-aid kit!

What happened to the dog that ate nothing but garlic?
His bark was much worse than his bite!

What do you get if you cross a dog with a Concorde?
A jet-setter!

What do you call a cat that has swallowed a duck?
A duck-filled fatty puss!

Did you hear about the cat that drank five bowls of water?
He set a new lap record!

Did you hear about the cat that swallowed a ball of wool?
She had mittens!

Dos and Don'ts of looking after dogs and cats

Dogs dos and don'ts

DO

- Be gentle and quiet around dogs at all times – treat them as you would like to be treated.
- Have respect for dogs.

DON'T

- Sneak up on a dog – you could scare them.
- Tease a dog – it's not fair.
- Stare at a dog – dogs can find this scary.
- Disturb a dog who is sleeping or eating.

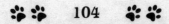

- Assume a dog wants to play with you. Just like you, sometimes they may want to be left alone.
- Approach a dog who is without an owner as you won't know if the dog is friendly or not.

Cats dos and don'ts

DO
- Be gentle and quiet around cats at all times.
- Have respect for cats.
- Let a cat approach you in their own time.

DON'T
- Stare at a cat as they can find this intimidating.

- Tease a cat – it's not fair.
- Disturb a sleeping or eating cat – they may not want attention or to play.
- Assume a cat will always want to play. Like you, sometimes they want to be left alone.

Some fun pet-themed puzzles!

Common Dog Breeds

Here is a list of some common dog breeds.
See if you can find them in the word search.
The words can be written backwards, diagonally,
forwards, up and down, so look carefully and
GOOD LUCK!

AMERICAN
BULLDOG
BEAGLE
DOBERMAN
GERMAN
SHEPHERD
GREYHOUND
JACK RUSSELL
AKITA
LABRADOR
LURCHER
MONGREL
ROTTWEILER
HUSKY
BULL TERRIER
SHIH TZU
SHAR PEI
BULLMASTIFF

```
W Q P J D G O D L L U B N A C I R E M A
A S Y D A W Q R D Z P L A F P K H G Q R
F E E W E C R S H S U X E W H O S J P E
F B C A T I K A G X Y E C F G B D Q Z I
I S M T G A X R O T T W E I L E R S S R
T B D R C V J K U Y F U H L U R C H E R
S I W V B T N W O S G E H I V X D A A E
A Q C L E E T K Y U S O A U Y F E R O T
M V D G R E A T F T H E R X H K I P F L
L A N Y J T R G J Q I G L L M L Z E I L
L Z U Z J K Y I L G H N N L E Z P I D U
U A O S D Y U H K E T J N B L R A Z E B
B J H U S K Y C G A Z B A F M K G I S E
J X Y X M Z D R H S U I M C N Q W N L F
M K E G K J I N C N M V R U O Y N L O W
E C R Q N W P K C T M J E Z M K P Q A M
B H G V D P X B L Z C O B I O Q O L S P
A Z T L R R L A B R A D O R O M B D A I
G S F W G C H S N P F G D M N C X T V O
G E R M A N S H E P H E R D P U O A S Z
```

Can you think of any other breeds? Write them in the spaces below.

Tangled Leads and Crazy Maze

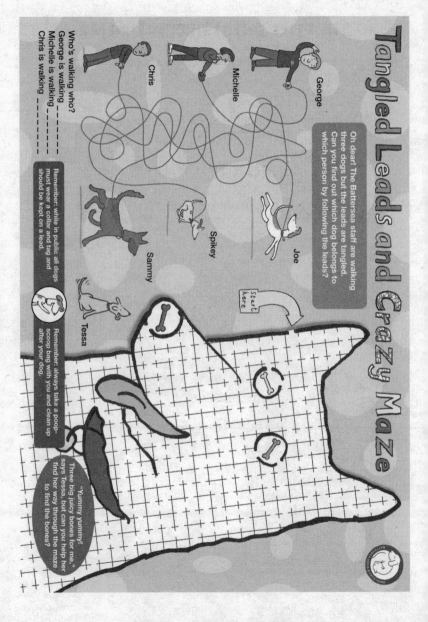

Oh dear! The Battersea staff are walking three dogs but the leads are tangled. Can you find out which dog belongs to which person by following the leads?

George

Michelle

Chris

Spikey

Joe

Sammy

Tessa

Start here

Who's walking who?
George is walking --------
Michelle is walking --------
Chris is walking --------

Remember while in public all dogs must wear a collar and tag and should be kept on a lead.

Remember always take a poop-scoop bag with you and clean up after your dog.

"Yummy yummy! Three big juicy bones for me," says Tessa, but can you help her find her way through the maze to find the bones?

Here is a delicious recipe for you to follow:

Remember to ask an adult to help you.

Cheddar Cheese Dog Cookies

You will need:

227g grated Cheddar cheese

(use at room temperature)

114g margarine

1 egg

1 clove of garlic (crushed)

172g wholewheat flour

30g wheatgerm

1 teaspoon salt

30ml milk

Preheat the oven to 375°F/190°C/gas mark 5.

Cream the cheese and margarine together. When smooth, add the egg and garlic and mix well. Add the flour, wheatgerm and salt. Mix well until a dough forms. Add the milk and mix again.

Chill the mixture in the fridge for one hour.

Roll the dough onto a floured surface until it is about 4cm thick. Use cookie cutters to cut out shapes.

Bake on an ungreased baking tray for 15–18 minutes.

Cool to room temperature and store in an airtight container in the fridge.

There are lots of fun things on the
website, including an online quiz,
e-cards, colouring sheets and recipes
for making dog and cat treats.

www.battersea.org.uk

Have you read all these books in the
Battersea Dogs & Cats Home series?

BAILEY'S story	**MAX'S** story	**RUSTY'S** story	**MISTY'S** story	**CHESTER'S** story
DAISY'S story	**HUEY'S** story	**STELLA'S** story	**SNOWY'S** story	**ANGEL'S** story
SUZY'S story	**ALFIE'S** story	**COSMO'S** story	**BUDDY** and **HOLLY'S** story	**COCO'S** story
SPARKLE and **BELLE'S** story	**BUSTER'S** story	**BRUNO'S** story	**JESSIE'S** story	**OSCAR'S** story
ROCKY'S story	**JAZZ** and **BO'S** story	**PIPPIN'S** story	**BERTIE'S** story	**PETAL'S** story